This edition published by Parragon in 2011
Parragon
Queen Street House
4 Queen Street
Bath BA1 1HE, UK

Based on the Mowgli Stories in *The Jungle Book*
and *The Second Jungle Book* by Rudyard Kipling.

ISBN 978-1-4454-2251-0
Printed in China.

Bath • New York • Singapore • Hong Kong • Cologne • Delhi
Melbourne • Amsterdam • Johannesburg • Auckland • Shenzhen

Long ago, deep in the jungles of India, there lived a wise black panther named Bagheera. One day, as Bagheera walked along the river, he saw something surprising – a baby! It was lying in a boat that had crashed onto the shore.

"Why, it's a Man-cub!" the panther said to himself.

The Man-cub desperately needed food. Bagheera took the baby to the den of a nearby wolf family. The mother had just had pups, and Bagheera hoped she would take care of the Man-cub.

The panther placed the baby near the den and stepped away. After a few quick sniffs, the mother wolf accepted the boy. She called him Mowgli and carried him into her den. Bagheera's plan had worked!

For ten years, Mowgli lived with the wolves, who treated him as one of their own.

Occasionally, Bagheera went to see how Mowgli was getting on. He seemed very happy, but Bagheera suspected that one day Mowgli would need to return to his own people in the Man-village.

Mowgli was a favourite among all the jungle animals. All, that is, except Shere Khan, a strong and cunning tiger.

Shere Khan feared nothing but Man's gun and Man's fire. He had heard of the young Man-cub and believed that Mowgli would grow up to be a hunter. Shere Khan wanted to make sure that did not happen.

One night, the wolf elders met at Council Rock to discuss the matter.

"He will surely kill the boy," Akela, the wolf leader, told the council. Then he announced that Mowgli would have to leave the jungle.

"But the boy can't find his way through the jungle alone!" protested one of the wolves.

"Maybe I can help you," offered Bagheera. "I know a Man-village, where he would be safe."

"So be it," said Akela, "There is no time to lose. Good luck!"

The very next day, Bagheera set out with Mowgli. They travelled fast, and deep into the jungle.

“We’ll spend the night here,” the panther said after a while.

The pair settled down to sleep on a tree branch. They were both very tired and drifted off to sleep quickly.

Just then, Kaa the snake appeared. He thought Mowgli would make a tasty treat.

Using his hypnotic eyes, Kaa put Mowgli in a trance. Then he wrapped the Man-cub in his coils.

Bagheera awoke and saw what was happening. He quickly jumped up and hit the snake on the head. Smack! With a bruised head and an empty belly, Kaa slithered away. Mowgli was safe – for now.

The next morning, Mowgli and Bagheera were awakened by a loud rumbling and shaking.

Bagheera covered his ears and groaned, “Oh no, the morning parade!”

“A parade!” Mowgli shouted enthusiastically. He grabbed a vine and swung down from the tree to take a look.

It was a parade of elephants! Colonel Hathi, their leader, was at the front, giving orders and keeping everyone in line.

Mowgli wanted to march like an elephant, too.

At the very end of the line, a baby elephant was marching proudly along. Mowgli ran up to him and asked, “May I join in?”

“Sure! Just copy everything I do,” nodded the little elephant.

Mowgli got down on all fours and marched along.

“Company, about turn!” ordered Colonel Hathi. But Mowgli continued marching in the same direction.

Bonk! Mowgli and the baby elephant bumped straight into each other!

“Company, halt!” cried Colonel Hathi.

All the elephants stood to attention for a troop inspection. Colonel Hathi walked along the line, inspecting one trunk after another. Mowgli tried to raise his nose as high in the air as he possibly could.

“What happened to your trunk?” thundered Colonel Hathi, when he saw Mowgli. He picked him up to take a closer look at him.

“Hey! You’re a Man-cub!” he cried in surprise. “What are you doing in my jungle?”

“This is not your jungle!” Mowgli replied indignantly.

At that moment, Bagheera appeared. “The boy is with me,” said the panther. “I’m taking him back to his village.”

“For good?” demanded Colonel Hathi.

“You have my word!” said Bagheera.

“Very well,” muttered the elephant. “But remember, elephants never forget!”

Bagheera insisted that they continue on their way to the Man-village. But Mowgli was having fun in the jungle and didn't want to leave.

"Then from now on, you're on your own," snapped the panther, losing his patience.

But as Bagheera watched Mowgli disappear into the jungle, he felt worried. "Foolish Man-cub," he sighed.

Mowgli trudged through the jungle and sat down by a rock for a rest. Just then, Baloo the bear happened to pass by.

"Hey! What a cute little Man-cub!" grinned Baloo, and sniffed Mowgli.

"What's it like to be a bear?" Mowgli asked Baloo.

Baloo decided to teach Mowgli the 'bare necessities' of life. He showed his young protégé how easy it was to find delicious treats in the jungle, such as bananas and coconuts. Mowgli was impressed. Being a bear sure looked like fun!

"Can I stay with you Baloo?" he asked.

"Sure, little buddy!" replied Baloo.

The two new friends jumped in the river and let themselves float downstream, singing a happy song.

"I would like to be a bear!" Mowgli sighed happily. Baloo patted him on the head.

"You can already sing like a bear!" he smiled.

Suddenly, a group of monkeys swooped down from the trees and grabbed Mowgli.

"Hey! Give me back my Man-cub!" shouted Baloo. But the monkeys ignored the bear and carried Mowgli off to their leader, King Louie.

King Louie lived deep in the jungle in a ruined city. He dreamed of being a human, and doing all the things that Man could do.

"I've heard that you would like to stay in the jungle. I can organize that for you," he promised Mowgli. "In return, I want you to tell me the secret of how people make fire."

"But I don't know how to make fire," said Mowgli, in surprise. This angered King Louie.

Meanwhile, Baloo had fetched Bagheera and they were hiding in the ruins nearby, listening to everything.

"You go down and create a distraction while I rescue Mowgli!" ordered Bagheera.

King Louie and his band of apes began to sing about being human, and dance the Boogie Woogie. Baloo disguised himself as an ape and joined in. When King Louie saw the new dancer, he seized Baloo's hand and began to dance with him.

In the meantime, Bagheera tried to rescue Mowgli from the gang of monkeys. But each time the boy came within his grasp, one of the monkeys would grab him again and whirl him away from the panther.

Suddenly, something awful happened! Baloo's disguise fell off as he danced, and all the monkeys realized they had been tricked.

The angry monkeys pounced on Baloo, and after a scuffle he started to run away.

"Baloo, take me with you!" shouted Mowgli.

So, a tug-of-war developed between Baloo and King Louie, with Mowgli in the middle. All the fighting caused the ruined city to start collapsing. While the monkeys tried to protect themselves from the falling rubble, Baloo, Bagheera and Mowgli managed to escape into the jungle.

"Boy, what a laugh!" Baloo chuckled.
But Bagheera didn't see the funny side.
"Mowgli can't survive in the jungle on his own. Sooner or later he will meet Shere Khan and the tiger will kill him. We need to get Mowgli to the Man-village where he will be safe with his own people."
With a heavy heart, Baloo saw that Bagheera was right.

But when Baloo tried to explain this to Mowgli, he couldn't understand why he had to leave.

"You're just as mean as Bagheera!" he cried, and ran off into the jungle.

Baloo and Bagheera searched for him in the jungle. Bagheera asked Colonel Hathi and his elephant troop to help him find Mowgli. Meanwhile, Shere Khan, the tiger, was lurking in the undergrowth nearby and overheard everything the panther said. He decided to find Mowgli for himself...

But someone had already found Mowgli – Kaa the snake! He had captured Mowgli and was trying to hypnotize him again.

But before Kaa's magic had time to work, Shere Khan, who had set off in search of the lost Man-cub, spotted the snake's tail dangling from a tree.

When he heard Kaa talking to someone, he grew suspicious and pulled on his tail.

"I'd like a few words with you," he purred.

“What a surprise!” said the snake, trying
› look innocent.

“Who were you speaking to, Kaa?” said
here Khan, stretching his long claws.

Wanting to keep Mowgli for himself, the
ıake pretended he hadn’t seen him, and
here Khan went on his way.

While Kaa and the tiger were talking, Mowgli managed to escape. He was finally free, but he felt sad and tired. The Man-cub sat down on a rock to rest.

Soon, four vultures flew down and started to tease him.

"What's up? You look like you haven't got a friend in the world!"

Mowgli shook his head sorrowfully.

When the vultures saw how lonely he was, they decided to be kinder. They said they would be his friend and made him an honorary vulture.

Suddenly, Shere Khan emerged from the undergrowth. “There’s my little Man-cub!” smiled the tiger cunningly. The vultures fled. But Mowgli didn’t move.

“You don’t scare me, Shere Khan!” said Mowgli, bravely.

When Mowgli went to attack the tiger with a stick, Shere Khan lunged at the Man-cub, his razor-sharp claws flashing.

But Baloo arrived just in time! The brave bear grabbed Shere Khan by the tail and pulled him away from his friend. Shere Khan pounced on Baloo. The vultures came back, picked up Mowgli and carried him to safety.

Suddenly, a bolt of lightning struck a nearby tree and set fire to it.

"Fire!" cried the vultures. "It's the only thing Shere Khan is afraid of!"

Mowgli picked up a burning branch and snuck up behind Shere Khan. He tied the branch to the tiger's tail.

Shere Khan suddenly noticed the flames behind him. Gripped by fear, the terrified tiger shot off into the jungle, never to be seen again.

As the vultures were congratulating themselves on their victory over Shere Khan, they noticed Mowgli kneeling on the ground over Baloo's body.

"Baloo! Stand up! Oh please, get up!" Mowgli cried desperately. But Baloo did not stir.

Bagheera tried to console him. Sadly they turned and walked away, thinking about what a good friend Baloo had been.

"Hey, what's happening?"

They suddenly heard Baloo's voice behind them! Overjoyed Mowgli sprang into his arms, shouting, "Baloo, you're alive!"

The three friends set off into the jungle once again. All of a sudden, the Man-cub heard a new and beautiful sound. He climbed a tree to investigate.

At a watering hole, a girl was singing as she braided her hair. Mowgli watched transfixed. But suddenly the branch on which he was sitting broke, and Mowgli fell with a splash into the water.

Laughing, the girl filled her jug and started to walk towards the Man-village. Then the jug slid from her hand and rolled at Mowgli's feet. Mowgli smiled at her, shyly.

"It looks as though Mowgli is going to like the Man-village, after all!" Baloo smiled.

Mowgli picked up the jug and started to follow the girl to the Man-village. He turned around one last time and threw a goodbye glance at his two friends, Bagheera and Baloo.

“I’ll miss that little fella,” sighed Baloo.

“Mowgli is where he belongs,” Bagheera consoled his friend.

Baloo smiled. “He would have made a very fine bear!”

The two turned and walked off into the jungle together, happy that Mowgli was safe at last.

The End